READY... SET... FROG!

To Dimitri, Petra, and Yanni, for your support and enthusiasm. —KM

To my mom, Lois Watson, for her endless encouragement and love. —LW

Published by Set Sail Press LLC
PO Box 145, Troy, MI 48099
info@setsailpress.com

Printed in the United States of America

Book design by Lindsay Broderick
Edited by Brooke Vitale

Library of Congress Control Number: 2022923916
Hardcover ISBN: 979-8-9874626-0-7
Paperback ISBN: 979-8-9874626-1-4
   E-book ISBN: 979-8-9874626-2-1

READY... SET... FROG!

Katharine Mitropoulos

Illustrated by **Laura Watson**

SET SAIL PRESS

Frogathan Spots—Frog for short—loved living on Harmony Lane. He loved creating new games to play with his neighbors. He loved building obstacle courses. And most of all, he loved *challenges*.

"Well, would you look at that," Frog's mom said one morning. "Harmony Lane is hosting a neighborhood fair next week. And there will be an obstacle course!"

Frog perked up. "An obstacle course? Really? I should practice!"

And before his mother could say another word, Frog went off to do just that.

Frog gathered every stone he could find in the backyard.
Then, one by one, he piled them into a tall mountain.

Soon Frog was ready to jump.

"Ready... set..."

FROG!

Mole's voice startled Frog, and he crashed into the rock pile. Stones and pebbles fell all around him.

It had taken so long to stack them up! What was he going to do now?

Frog turned toward the fence. "Is everything okay, Mole?"

"I'm making apple pie, and I'm one apple short. Could you please hop to the top of my tree and get an apple for me?"

Frog really wanted to rebuild the mountain so he could practice, but his friend needed his help. That was more important than a contest, **wasn't it?**

Frog took a deep breath. He focused his eyes on the tallest branch, then he bent his knees.

His feet pushed off, and he soared into the air. The wind whipped his face as he glided up, up, up.

Even if he wasn't practicing,
he did love hopping!

Frog hopped this way
and that, searching for
the perfect apple.

Then he saw it:
the brightest,
plumpest apple
on the whole tree.

"Thank you, Frog!
I'll be sure to bring you a slice when the pie is done."

The next morning, Frog went back outside to practice.
"Today is the day!" he cheered.

First, he balanced sticks between two chairs to create a bridge.

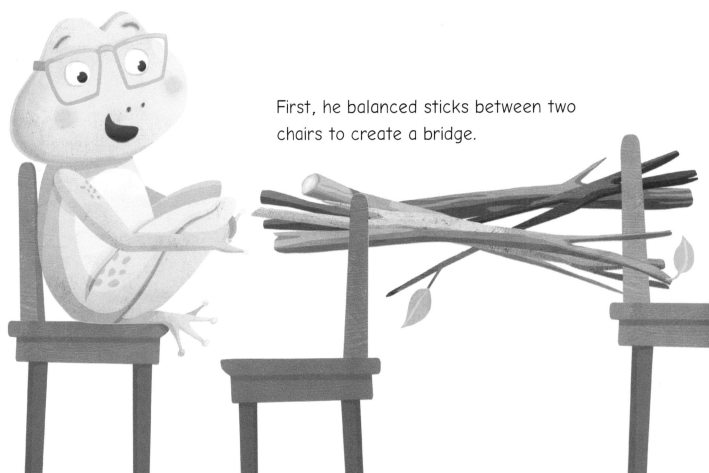

Next, he piled stone upon stone to build his rock mountain.

"Ready... set..."

FROG!

Frog lost his balance and tipped into his obstacle. Down went the chair, **and down went his bridge!**

Giraffe's long neck craned over the fence.

"Frog, could you help me put on my hat?
It's awfully sunny this morning."

Frog's cheeks burned. He had worked so hard on his bridge, and now the sticks were all over the yard! Nothing was going his way!

But his friend needed his help.

Giraffe's long neck swayed back and forth. Frog balanced as he moved her hat this way and that.

"Too high," Giraffe complained. "Too low. Too high again—the sun is in my eyes. Wait—now I can't see anything!"

At last, Giraffe was happy. "Thanks, Frog! That's just right!"

On the way home from school, Frog wanted to practice jumping from stone to stone.

"Ready... set..." FROG!

Looking around, he spotted Kitten across the pond.

"Help, Frog!
I was playing on the lily pads
and I got stuck over here."

Frog still needed to rebuild his obstacle course so he could practice before it got dark. Hopping to the other side of the pond and back would take forever!

Frog looked all around to see if anyone else could help, but it was just him.

So he hopped from
lily pad

to **lily pad**

until he
reached Kitten.

That night, Frog pushed his food sadly around his plate.
"Mom, I don't want to enter the contest anymore.
I haven't had any time to practice."

Frog's mother smiled down at him. "How did you help Mole?"

"I jumped into the tree to get an apple."

"And Giraffe?" Mom asked.

"I balanced on her neck to put on her hat. And I hopped from lily pad to lily pad to help Kitten..."

"You see, you've been practicing all along. Just not the way you planned to."

"It was kind of you to help your friends. But remember, it's OK to say no sometimes. It takes practice to balance helping yourself and helping others. I'm still working on it too!"

Frog thought about his day. "It felt good to help my friends. But maybe next time, I can save some time for my own plans too."

At the fair, Frog lined up with his friends.

When the whistle blew, he hopped up the

stack of logs,

across the wobbly
**bridge
of hay,**

and from **rock
to rock.**

At bedtime, Frog smiled proudly at his second-place trophy. Even though he hadn't won, he was excited for next year... and maybe if he took some time for himself, **things would go a little more like he planned.**

About the Author

Katharine is a wife and a mom of two who lives with her family in Michigan. Katharine is a trained speech-language pathologist whose degrees in psychology, speech-language pathology, and linguistics sparked her interest in children's literature. When she's not writing books about Frog and his friends, you can find Katharine building furniture in her family woodshop, eating ice cream with rainbow sprinkles, or running road races all over the state.

About the Illustrator

Laura Watson lives and works in downtown
Toronto, Ontario, with her husband, teenage
daughter, and a big orange dog named Red.
A childhood spent drawing, painting, and making
crafts led to art school to pursue studies in
fine art and illustration. Since then, Laura has
created lighthearted and whimsical illustrations
for children's books and magazines, textiles and
stationery, and various children's toys and puzzles.
Laura works in her cozy studio tucked in a corner
of a 130-year-old Gothic Revival office building
that may or may not be haunted. In her spare
time, she runs at the beach, reads, and takes
long, adventurous walks with her dog.

Ingram Content Group UK Ltd.
Milton Keynes UK
UKHW050003170423
420274UK00001B/1